Investi GATORS
Off the Hook

written and illustrated by
John Patrick Green

with colour by **Aaron Polk**

MACMILLAN CHILDREN'S BOOKS

To Steve, Heidi, Amy
and the rest of the DA crew.

First published in the US 2021 by First Second
First published in the UK 2021 by Macmillan Children's Books

This edition published in the UK 2022 by Macmillan Children's Books
an imprint of Pan Macmillan
The Smithson, 6 Briset Street, London EC1M 5NR
EU representative: Macmillan Publishers Ireland Limited,
Mallard Lodge, Lansdowne Village, Dublin 4
Associated companies throughout the world
www.panmacmillan.com

ISBN 978-1-5290-6609-8

1 3 5 7 9 8 6 4 2

A CIP catalogue record for this book is available from the British Library.

Cover design by John Patrick Green and Kirk Benshoff
Interior book design by John Patrick Green
Interior colour by Aaron Polk

Printed in China by Leo Paper

Chapter 1

Under cover of night...

chugga chugga chugga chugga chugga

...a train speeds along a mountain pass!

Tickets?

Tickets?

chugga chugga chugga chugga chu

Tickets?

And **ALSO** undercover on that train are the...

AAAH!

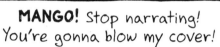

MANGO! Stop narrating! You're gonna blow my cover!

BOOP

Sorry, Brash...

You know how much I like trains. I just got carried away!

Remember, *your* cover is to keep the train running safely...

EMERGENCY BRAKE

...but we're *undercover* because **someone** on this train carries a case with a **stolen list** of S.U.I.T.* agents' names. So keep your eyes peeled for any clues.

Clues to a S.U.I.T.case, right. Like I'm just gonna find...

...a trail of...bread crumbs?

And until then, maintain radio silence!

OOF!

*Special Undercover Investigation Teams

3

6

There's not enough time to do both, so choo-choo-choose wisely!

Chapter 2

Deep inside S.U.I.T. Headquarters...

TRAINING SIMULATOR

fssh

RAINING SIMULAT

tap tap tap

Mango, you've run that training simulation a dozen times and you *still* haven't got it right.

It's not fair, Brash! It's a **no-win scenario!**

Even if I let Crackerdile *kill you* and I get to the front of the train *before* he bombs the bridge, the brakes are out, and we all go over the cliff anyway.

It always ends the same: Everyone dies and Crackerdile gets away!

Have you tried...*not* saving me **OR** stopping the train, but *just* capturing Crackerdile?

But...you're my partner! You'd die — and so would all the passengers!

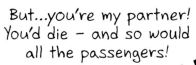

True. But you've got to think about the **GREATER GOOD.**

Crackerdile is a threat to **thousands**, maybe **MILLIONS** of people — maybe even the **WHOLE WORLD!** No matter what happens to me or the people on that train, if he *gets away*, the mission is a *failure!*

What do you mean he's a threat to thousands? Last time we saw him he was a **pile of mush** that probably got washed out to sea. I don't even know why I'm training to stop him.

EIGNING SIMULATOR

DRAINING SI

You're right. Crackerdile *ISN'T* a threat anymore. But if you can't beat *him,* what if there's a villain even *MORE* dangerous than a former-agent-turned-radioactive-cracker?

Plus, there's more to learn from this simulation than just how to stop Crackerdile. Like how to make tough decisions in the heat of the moment.

It's a skill that would make *ME* the **PERFECT FIELD AGENT!**

≥sigh≤

Buuuuuut it **does** also come in handy when thinking up spy scenarios to test **OTHER** agents' skills.

Ah! There you are, Gators!

What is it, C-ORB*?

I have an urgent update on – **Oh!** Hello, Cilantro. I didn't see you there.

*Computerized Ocular Remote Butler

HA HA! I'm kidding. I'm a giant unblinking eyeball. I see *everything*!

EVERYTHING.

Mango, this says we need to head to the Science Factory, ASAP! It's about the **Bill Plungerman** case!

You mean the case of the missing plumber whose *arm* was combined with a *snake*, giving him grappling hook powers?

We've been trying everything to find him.

I even set alerts tracking every social media hashtag I can think of.

< ALERT TERMS
#PlumberSnake
#SnakePlumber
#SnakeArmedMan
#ManTailedSnake
#ArmSnake
#SnakeArm
#WhatsSnakin

⸮AHEM⸮ You're *also* late for your appointment with **Sven Septapus** in the A.R.M.S.* Division to try on the prototype V.E.S.T.s he's developed.

Right! New V.E.S.T.s, then on to the Science Factory. Thanks, C-ORB. C'mon, Mango!

Uh... Bye, I guess.

*Apparel Research and Manufacturing...Service? Section? Something?

23

Why always *vests?* Why not something like... a *trench coat?* Trench coats are **way cool**... So **mysterious**...

You can never tell if someone's a **GOOD GUY** or a **BAD GUY** if they're in a trench coat!

We're **GOOD GUYS** no matter *what* we wear, Mango...

But we are **In-VEST-igators**, not **In-TRENCH COAT-igators**. That doesn't even make sense!

Chapter 3

26

Welcome back, **Hookline** and **Slinker**...

...my favourite (and only) member — uh, *members?* — of my evil team, **T.A.I.L.BLAZERS!**

Our mission: the Total Annihilation of Idiot Law-doers!

And who knows what kind of effect microwaves would have on the **radioactive waste** that courses through my veins...if I even have veins...

Bah! None of this junk will help me, **CRACKERDILE**, be restored from this bucket of dough back to my crispy, crackery condition.

rub rub

Not that that crumby carcass was ever all it was cracked up to be.

32

Chapter 4

I've gotta admit, it's nice to find someone in a predicament similar to my own.

Me, a villanous bucket of unbaked batter. You, a monstrous, plumber-tailed snake. Both of us on a quest for revenge!

I assume! Correct me if I'm wrong, but revenge is a common motivation for villains and monsters.

Hey, what's this? The abandoned opera house! That's both grand *AND* epic! Hmm... Looks like it's seen better days, but it may have potential for a secret lair.

Gah! Nasty! Shoo! *SHOO!!*

This place is definitely a *fixer-upper*. You may be a plumber, but we'll need a *lot* more help — like a bunch of construction workers to repair that roof.

Pigeon poop is one thing, but if we find a way to re-bake me *back* into a cracker, I certainly can't risk getting rained on!

CLOSED

flrp

Chapter 5

Back at S.U.I.T. HQ...

Sven! The InvestiGators are here!

Sven?

A.R.M.S.
APPAREL RESEARCH and MANUFACTUR

HEY, SVEN!

Huh. Where could he be?

Hello, Mango and Brash. Sven's just finishing up. I'm Aiden. This is Nine.

Oh! Hello, Agents Eight and Nine.

*Very Exciting Spy Technology

Indeed you are, Brash! Previously you needed a different V.E.S.T. for each new undercover job. But now...

BOOP

COOL! I wanna try it out!

Be my guest!

Toss

Button

Button

I'm sorry, Cilantro, but I didn't get the idea from you. Yes, you're a chameleon, but octopuses can change their colour and texture, too.

Bip

I've been perfecting this technology for as long as I can remember.

But...but...

I thought the plural of *octopus* was *octopi...?*

Mmm, pie.

blurp

InvestiGators!
Where are you on the Bill Plungerman case?

vvrp

C-ORB gave you that file **25 pages ago!** You should be at the Science Factory by now!

Oh! Yes, sir, General Inspector. On our way!

vrrp

C'mon, Brash! Put on your new V.E.S.T.!

Wait — you're actually wearing *my* new V.E.S.T., Mango. That's the colour brown that *I* always wear.

Just put on the other one.

You can make 'em any colour you want. See?

bip

bip

Remember, Gators, those V.E.S.T.s are *PROTOTYPES!*

They haven't been field tested yet!

Now, Cilantro...

Cilantro?

Chapter 6

There! Head into that trailer.

Hashtag dis... Hashtag dat...

WHAM

CONSTRUCTION MAN!

Dat's **FOREman.** What can I do you for?

I'd like to hire your crew for a quick fix-'em-up job.

Chapter 7

Meanwhile...

SCIENCE FACTORY

Ah, Mango and Brash! Welcome back to the Science Factory.

WELCOME to the WORLD of SCIENCE!

Thanks, Dr! It's nice to be here when you're not in the middle of a **science accident!**

Give it time. This is only page 54!

Yes, their bodies were combined. But now their *one body* has TWO HEADS! And as the **Head Scientist**, I can tell you that two heads aren't always better than one!

Two heads means two *BRAINS*, and it's my guess that the brain of the snake and the brain of the plumber are fighting for control over their combined body.

That must be what's made Bill Plungerman so hard to find. Who could predict what a snake brain might do with a plumber body?

I've discovered another wrench in the works. Well, not a *wrench*, but a different tool—

The plumber's **DRAIN SNAKE TOOL!**

That's right. Bill was here to unclog a drain. But *tools* don't have *brains*, Dr.

I saw on security footage from the incident that the snake was wrapped around the tool *and* the plumber's arm at the moment they all got combined.

That tool must be how the snake-arm got grappling hook powers!

With power like that, the snake and/or plumber might not **want** to be found!

OR cured! And uncombining their bodies and minds won't be easy. There's a huge risk of the plumber getting the snake's mind or vice versa.

And one of them could still be combined with the drain snake tool!

But if I can invent a device that can hold both of their minds, we could extract their consciousnesses before we uncombine their bodies — and make sure the right mind winds up in the right body afterwards!

Well, first we need to find this plumber-snake combo. Right, Mango?

Mango?

61

Chapter Aiden—I MEAN—8

Now repair the roof on my **secret lair**—*I MEAN*—the **opera house!**

Yeah, okays. I can schedule your job in, uh...six months.

Scroll scroll Scroll

WHADDYA MEAN YOU'LL DO THE JOB IN SIX MONTHS?!

No, no. I didn't say dat.

I said I can *schedule* da job in six months.

Meaning, in half a year I can looks at my *calendar*, and *DEN* I can find a time dat my crew can do your job.

So you're probably lookin' at a **whole year** from now 'fore we can get to it.

Well, *that's* taken care of. Now to recruit more members to **T.A.I.L.Blazers!** We can use all this money to print flyers!

But wait... No one's going to want to join a team led by a *soft pile of mush.* I need to pull myself together...make something outta myself. I've gotta get TOUGH! **BULK UP!**

Hold on! I saw just the place when we robbed that bank!

Take me to... THE **MAW!**

Chapter 9

Thanks, ma'am. We'll see what we can dough. I mean, see what we can **do**.

I – I need to freshen up after all this excitement!

OH! Excuse me! You, uh, may want to give it a minute in there, if you know what I mean.

So, what happened during the robbery?

You can tell us. We're *professionals*.

Well, since you're both investment bankers... A guy showed up with a bucket of dough and demanded *MORE* dough!

By "dough" you mean money? So he had money and wanted *more* money?

siiip

He had **dough** and he wanted **money**. He told me to put the **money** in the bucket of **dough!**

Riiiiight, okay. And you put the **dough** in the bucket he had for the **money?**

No! I put the **money** in the bucket he had for the **dough**!

Isn't that exactly what I said?

What did this guy look like?

I didn't actually get a good look at him. He was disguised by a big trench coat and—

GASP! BRASH! You know who likes to rob banks and disguise himself with big coats?!

HOUDINO, THE DINOSAUR ESCAPE ARTIST!

Why'd you hang up?

Mango, if he's in prison, then he's **not** the guy in the trench coat!

Oh, right.

click

Well?

Sorry, man, they hung up!

Hmmm...

That was a dead end.

Why are investment bankers calling prisoners?

Oh! Er, we were just, uh...

Okay, here's the truth: As investment bankers, which we are, we meet a lot of *criminals* in our line of work, which is investment banking, and—

MANGO!

What?

HA HA! Speaking of criminals, is there anything else you can remember about this guy in the trench coat? You know, for, uh, investment banking purposes?

Yeah, before the funny one brought up dinosaurs, I was going to say that he had a **snake** for an **arm.**

THE SNAKE-ARMED MAN!

Was this snake-arm attached to a *plumber* by any chance?

Uh, I really couldn't tell.

Hmm, then there's no way to be certain *THIS* is the same snake-armed man we're looking for.

Mango, how many snake-armed men do you think there are?!

OF COURSE this is the one we're looking for.

Shouldn't we get back to work? I'm pretty sure our breaks are over by now.

Yes, right! Back to business! And there's no place investment bankers do **business** better than in the **bathroom!**

C'mon, Mango!

Chapter 10

Down there! **THE MAW!**

LAND!

This is where people go to *BULK UP!*

The **MOTHER** of **ALL WAFFLES!**

MOTHER of ALL WAFFLES

MAW

DRIVE-THRU 'ROUND BACK

Okay.

Boop

Here you are, sir! One medium waffle!

!

NO, you fools! Make *ME* a *WAFFLE!* I want to *BE* a *WAFFLE!*

Ooooohhh... Would you like to be one of our novelty shapes?

Ooh! I didn't think about that. Do you have...a *star* shape? Or maybe... a *dinosaur?*

No, we have... square...or... round.

Chapter 11

Wh-Who?

HISSSSSSSSSSSSSSSSSSSSS!

≥Gasp!≤

It's the **InvestiGators**, **Mango** and my former partner **Brash**!

I don't think they've seen me...

I can't take them on yet. I may have *kicked the bucket*, so to speak, but now I'm just a *medium-sized waffle!*

I need to be BIGGER, like the waffle on the roof!

Wait a sec...

That gives me an idea!

DRIVE-
THRU
ROUND
BACK

Bill... Robbing that bank was obviously a cry for help. If you come with us, we will find a cure for you and your arm.

Bill?

Hissssssssss name isss **HOOKLINE**...

...and **SSSSSLINKER!**

It seems the Head Scientist was right that the two brains are fighting for control.

Clearly, the **snake** is doing all the thinking!

And it's thinking *BAD THOUGHTS!*

98

Are you *mad* that I saved you?

I'm not mad, just...*disappointed.* Stopping the **bad guy** is the mission, not saving your partner.

You mean like how *YOU* didn't save your partner **Daryl** from falling into *radioactive dough* and turning into **Crackerdile?**

Excuse me for not wanting my partner to presumably *die* only to come back flattened and looking for *revenge!*

I – I'm sorry, Brash... That was a low blow.

No, Mango. You're right.

Sometimes looking out for your partner *is* the mission.

After all, I've had to look out for *you*, since you're always one step away from blowing our cover. *AND* I've had to keep a lookout for Daryl ever since he became evil.

Well... I guess I don't have to look out for *THAT* partner anymore, since he's gone forever.

Brash—

Being a secret agent isn't easy, Mango. I've had to make a lot of tough decisions for the **Greater Good.** You will, too.

MOTHER of ALL WAFFLES

Wh–Where are you going?

MAW

I'm going inside to see if the employees can tell me why Hookline and Slinker had such a craving for waffles that they had to rob a bank.

Plus, that giant waffle shouldn't have fallen over. Something's not adding up, and it's my mission to find out what.

Perhaps you want to think about *your* mission out here for a while.

Another hashtag alert...!

Bleep Blurp

Chapter 12

That certainly was exciting!

I *love* a good action scene!

But at this size, I'm no match for the InvestiGators.

Hookline and Slinker, go back to the opera house and make sure the construction workers – *HOLD ON...*

sneeeak

There's *got* to be someone or something in this place that can **EMBIGGEN** me...

WHOA!

That's the biggest chicken I've ever seen!

Of course, at *this* size, **everything** looks bigger than I've ever seen!

But as a **crocodile** who turned into a **cracker** who turned into a **waffle**, I've got a little experience with things that are *abnormal!*

He's **GOT** to know some science that will make me bigger.

SIP

DOINK

Chapter 13

Back at the MAW...

What a mess. Well, at least we recovered the stolen money...

≥AHEM!≤

Oh, uh...

I was just making sure it was all there!

Right...

shove

Now, does anyone know why the snake-armed man came into the MAW?

He wanted us to make him a waffle.

So he was just buying waffles with the money he stole from the bank?

No, we made the *DOUGH* into a waffle.

The *dough?* You mean you made waffles out of the *money?*

Not "money" dough. He had a bucket of **actual** dough! Like baking dough.

Bucket. Of. Dough.

Yep.

300 likes

CRACKERDILE!

Cracker? No, that's a *WAFFLE.*

WAFFLEDILE!

MANGO!

MANGO!

Mango? Where could he be?

I've got to warn him that **Crackerdile** is back! And he's a *WAFFLE!*

Wait! I can reach him on my V.E.S.T.!

Beep

Mango? MANGO?

ksh

ksh

Beep *Beep*

DRAT! Still on the fritz!

Hold on... If Hookline and Slinker brought Crackerdile to the MAW to be made into a waffle...then Crackerdile must be the one calling the shots!

HE'S the mastermind behind the bank robbery!

THAT'S what the bank teller meant by "bucket of dough"! How could I be so dense?

Smack

Crackerdile couldn't have needed *ALL* that money to get *waffle-ized*... So what was it for?

I should head back to the bank in case I missed any clues.

Chapter 14

Yeah, this place *does* need work.

But what would a snake-armed plumber want with an opera house?

Are these repairs what Hookline and Slinker robbed that bank for?

Gonna be tough paying these construction workers since they left the money at the MAW!

This is Cici Boringstories, reporting LIVE outside the **Mother of All Waffles!** According to the *Action News Now* police scanner, the chicken and waffle who escaped the Science Factory are *INSIDE* the restaurant!

This could be a **hostage situation!**

Officer! Do you think this incident has anything to do with the bank robbery? Or the #SnakeArmedMan who's trending on **teh interwebs?**

Well, I don't know about hashtags, but I **do** know about hash **browns!** They're *delicious*, and the MAW's got 'em for £1.99!

128

Chapter 15

Back to Brash...

Dagnabbit!
No additional clues in the bank, *AND* I left the MAW in such a hurry I forgot to bring back the stolen money!

But of greater concern, still no sign of Mango!

V.E.S.T., find Mango!

Nothing? Why can't it find him?

He's not in the bank, not at the MAW... Maybe he went back to S.U.I.T. Headquarters?

Wait a minute – when we left A.R.M.S., Mango technically took *MY* V.E.S.T.!

V.E.S.T.! Find *BRASH!*

pff

HOOKLINE and SLINKER?!

Since they're working with Crackerdile, then these flyers mean...

...they're *littering!*

crumple!

But more importantly, it means Crackerdile is putting together a team of **EVIL VILLAINS!** And he's using the opera house as a *not-so-secret lair!*

I still don't know where Mango went... but my mission is and will always be STOPPING CRACKERDILE! I **have** to stick with the mission!

Chapter 16

BLOOP

BATHROOM

HOUD

Lotta construction workers. Too busy to notice me...

≶GASP!≶ Dr. Doodledoo is working with Crackerdile!

Huh? **MANGO!** He's...*undercover* as a construction worker! What a relief. Smart move, partner!

Wait a minute – *HIS* eyes are all squiggly, too!

Mango and Dr. Doodledoo are ***HYPNOTIZED!***

Their hypnosis must be because of...

SLINKER, the SNAKE!

Science says snakes being able to hypnotize their prey is a *myth*... but Mango's eyes say science is *mythtaken!*

142

Mango and **Brash**. Nice of you to drop in. You're just in time for my *big moment!*

And by that I mean my *EMBIGGENING MOMENT!*

With this **EMBIGGEN DEVICE,** I, Waffledile, will become the *biggest evil waffle in the world!*

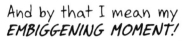

Then I will once and for all **squash** you **InvestiGators** like the insignificant ants you are!

HEY! That's offensive to *ants!*

145

Chapter 17

Crackerdile is back, and now he's a giant **WAFFLEDILE!** Can you believe it, Mango?

I thought I was just seeing things! Turns out I *WAS* seeing things, but *NOW* I'm believing things!

Uh... Brash? Slinker is coming to...

So is Hookline – I mean, Bill!

Wh-Who am I?

You're **Bill Plungerman, Ace Plumber!**

Wh-What have I done?!

What have WEEE DONE...

Don't look, Brash! Keep your eyes *shut!*

I'm **Mango** and this is **Brash**, by the way. We're **InvestiGators.**

Thanks. I...I think I remember you now, from that waffle place.

I know you tried to stop me. I didn't *WANT* to rob that bank... or hypnotize anyone... or learn Photoshop just so I could design those flyers...but I couldn't control myself. It's like I was a *puppet,* and this snake was *pulling the strings.*

Well, we now know that **CRACKERDILE** was the puppet master all along!

Speaking of whom, any idea where he'd go? What his plans are?

BRASH! I see him! Head downtown!

We're comin' for you, **WAFFLEDILE!**

VROOM VROOM

Chapter 18

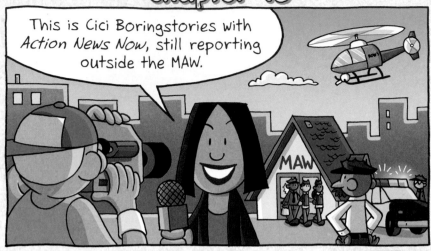

This is Cici Boringstories with *Action News Now*, still reporting outside the MAW.

Officer! Is there an update in the situation involving the chicken and waffle who escaped the Science Factory and are reportedly holding hostages inside?

Oh, yeah!

Turns out it was these *teenagers* who were holding the **chicken** and **waffles** hostage!

We're innocent employees!

*Translation: "I can't move!"

Why are we still under arrest? Haven't you realized the **giant waffle** on the **roof** is the one you were after?

He's the one that stole that money and kidnapped the chicken! Even us teenagers figured *that* out!

Well, I *guess* that makes sense...

But I hope you kids learned your lesson!

un-cuff

You heard it here first, viewers! The **snake-armed man** turned out to be a good guy, the **stolen bank money** has been recovered, the **waffle** has turned to stone, and the **chicken** has, presumably, been eaten!

Hold on... Correction: Only the chicken that was on the *MENU* has been eaten, *NOT* the one from the Science Factory. For *Action News Now*, this is Cici Boringstories, signing off.

*AAAAAAND...*we're out.

You didn't say anything about our **news copter** transforming into a **brain surgeon.**

Oh, *please.* No one's going to believe *THAT.*

It sounds like something straight out of a comic book!

Chapter 19

If you'll recall, way back on page 57, I had the idea to invent a device that can **harness the consciousnesses** of the plumber and the snake, to aid in the separation of their bodies.

I was mucking about with the chicken, but I'll take your word for it.

I am positive that if Dr. Hardbones and I put our minds together, we can use that technology to get Brash to wake up.

Just don't *ACTUALLY* put your minds together, because that's how this mess started in the first place!

Well, it sounds like Brash's brain is in good hands.

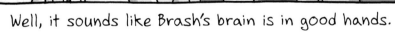

Indeed, it is! And **I** should know.

Mango...

Hookline and Slinker! I mean — Bill Plungerman...

Sorry.

No, that's okay. Is Brash... all right?

He's — He will be. Thank you for pulling him out of the belly of that big, bad, breakfasty beast.

Well, thanks to the **InvestiGators**, I'm no longer under that waffle's *OR* Slinker's control. And now I know how to snap out of the hypnosis, so I'll be able to keep from losing my head again.

There you are! So *THIS* is where everyone went!

Huff Huff

Dr. Doodledoo! Did you get lost?

This dude took off into the air when we were on our way to the Science Factory! It took me this long to catch up. I can't *fly,* you know. I'm a **chicken!**

Sorry about that. For giving you the slip, I mean. Not sorry that you're a chicken.

We're cool, bruh.

I just couldn't let Brash become a statue after saving me. Especially since all this trouble was my fault.

I want to make things right.

In fact, I might keep this snake-arm. The Head Scientist offered to separate us, but I think there's a lot of *GOOD* that **Hookline** and **Slinker** can do for the world.

Plus, this arm will **really** come in handy when I'm unclogging drains! I am a **plumber,** after all.

Epilogue

Thank you for coming in, Agent Mango.

I want to commend you on stopping **Crackerdile** – *er,* **Waffledile.**

GI MOE

Though he is *technically* still at large – **VERY** large – we at least know where he is, and he won't be going anywhere anytime soon.

Thank you, sir. But I still feel like Crackerdile **won.** What he — **I** — did to Brash...

Don't be too hard on yourself, Mango. You were faced with a tough decision, and you made the right call.

And while Brash is recovering, *YOU* are now S.U.I.T.'s **top agent.** There's a lot of crime out there that needs investigating.

TOP AGENT? I dunno, sir—

You won't be in the field alone, Mango. For the time being, you'll be paired up with a *NEW* partner... Just until Brash is back on his feet.

New... partner?

Even though Dr. Hardbones is still figuring out a way to wake up Brash, the Head Scientist was able to send me **downloads** of most of Brash's *personality* and *experiences*.

Then I uploaded them into this **robotic copy** I made out of spare parts.

No one's given up on the *real* Brash, Mango. RoboBrash is not a replacement for him.

But for now, out of **all** the other agents in S.U.I.T., no one would make a better partner for you than **RoboBrash!**

MONOCLE made the partner, technically.

So I'm...**not** his new partner...?

How about that, eh, Cilantro?

...Cilantro?

192

INVESTIGATORS

How to draw **WAFFLEDILE**

1. Start with a tall oval for his body. It doesn't have to be perfect!

2. Add some big curves for his forehead, with some smaller loops for his snout. Then erase the line where his head overlaps his body (shown in blue).

3. Draw arms with little triangles for fingers. Waffledile normally has three, but when he makes a fist you'll also see his thumb.

4. Next, add legs, with more triangles for toes. Include lines to show where his feet bend at the ankle.

5. Add details like eyes, nostrils, a mouth with pointy teeth and a grid for a waffle pattern.

6. Draw lines around one side of his nose, head, body, arms, and legs. This will make him look 3D but also flat! Erase a tiny bit of the lines where his arms and legs connect to his body.

7. Finally, colour him in. And give him some angry eyebrows, because Waffledile's always mad about something!

8. BONUS STEP! Pour maple syrup on him to turn Waffledile into a tasty treat!

WHAT? *NO!* Now I'm all *sticky!*

New Specials!

Free Delivery!

MAW

MOTHER of ALL WAFFLES

Wac 'n' Cheese

Two of our signature waffles with baked-in macaroni and cheese centres! They're ooey, gooey and make your tastebuds go kablooey! Served with maple sriracha.

Boneless Buffalo Wafflings

Half waffle, half wing, ALL FLAVOUR! Choice of mild, medium, hot or **volcano**. Served with celery and a smoked maple blue cheese dip. May contain bones.

Waldorffle Salad

A harmonious blend of apples, celery, grapes and wafflenuts, dressed in maple mayo, and served on a bed of wafflettuce.

The Chucket™

Chunks of buttermilk fried chicken served in an edible waffle-bucket! Available in small, medium and super-double-medium.

Menu subject to change without warning

The horror! THE HORROR!

200

Agent Monocle is hacking into a secret database and has one last chance to crack the code. Of the numbers she's tried below, each guess has just one correct digit that's in the correct order. Knowing that, can you figure out the 3-digit passcode?

Passcode: 896 ✗
Passcode: 983 ✗
Passcode: 246 ✗
Passcode: 843 ✗
Passcode: ✱✱✱ ✓

C-ORB sees everything, but he can't see the connection between these nine objects. Can you tell what they have in common, and work out if anything's missing?

*Go to **InvestiGatorsBooks.com** to check your answers!*

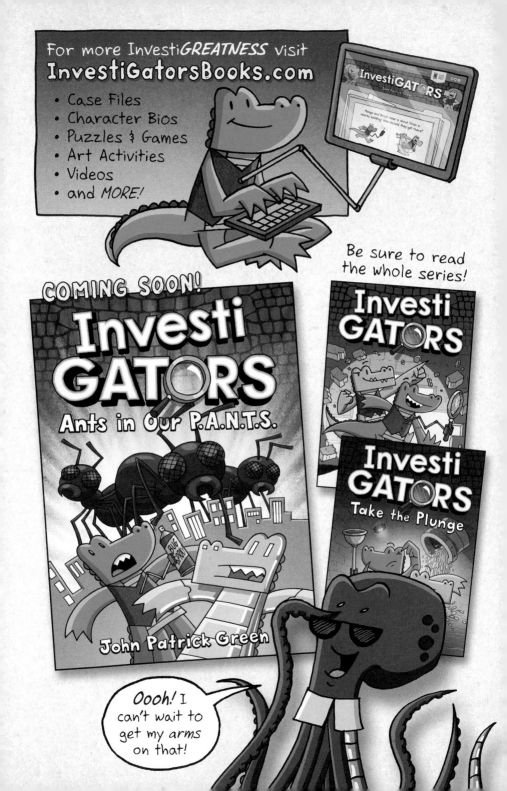

Invent a V.E.S.T.*!

Mango and RoboBrash! I put out the call for *new, creative, extra-special* V.E.S.T.s and our junior agents really delivered! This **SCENT DETECTOR** gadget was invented by **Clara** from **Grand Junction, Colorado.** Just provide a sample of something you want to find and it will track it by its *smell!*

Scent Detector: find me more bean tacos!

Zip zip zop

Sniff Sniff Sniff

It must be malfunctioning. This doesn't make sense!

Wrong! Mango's belly is *FULL* of beans. It *definitely* makes *scents!*

Sniff

HA HA HA!

*Very Exciting Spy Technology

Do you have an idea for a V.E.S.T.? Share it with us with #InvestigatorsBooks!

Special thanks to...

Aaron Polk and his flatters, Christine Brunson
and Robin Fasel, for their incredible colours.
My editors, Calista Brill, Rachel Stark,
and some new person, plus everyone else
at First Second who's had to tolerate me.
My agent, the extraordinary Jen Linnan.
All the movies, TV shows, songs, books,
etc. that I've lovingly paid homage to.
Dave Roman, Rich Zimmer,
and the rest of Cryptic Press.
And of course, my brother, Bill,
and the rest of my family.

John Patrick Green is a *New York Times*-bestselling author who makes books about animals with human jobs, such as *Hippopotamister*, the Kitten Construction Company series, and the InvestiGators series. John is definitely not just a bunch of animals wearing a human suit pretending to have a human job. He is also the artist and co-creator of the graphic novel series Teen Boat!, with writer Dave Roman. John lives in Brooklyn in an apartment that doesn't allow animals other than the ones living in his head.